To the children of Egypt – J.P.W.
To my god-daughter Kate – F.F.

Text copyright © 1994 by Jill Paton Walsh
Illustrations copyright © 1994 by Fiona French

First published in Great Britain by Frances Lincoln Limited,
4 Torriano Mews, Torriano Avenue, London NW5 2RZ

Printed in Italy

First U.S. Edition 1995
1 2 3 4 5 6 7 8 9 10

Library of Congress Cataloging in Publication Data
Paton Walsh, Jill.
Pepi and the secret names / by Jill Paton Walsh : illustrated by
Fiona French.
p.   cm.
Summary: As he paints the lion, hawk, crocodile, and cobra that
his son has managed to coax to serve as models for the decorations
on the tomb of Prince Dhutmose, Pepi's father captures an even more
important animal.
ISBN 0-688-13428-9 (RTE)
[1. Egypt–Fiction. 2. Animals–Fiction. 3. Cats–Fiction.]
I. French, Fiona, ill. II. Title.
PZ7.P2735P₈   1994   93-48620
[E]–dc20   CIP
                                                AC

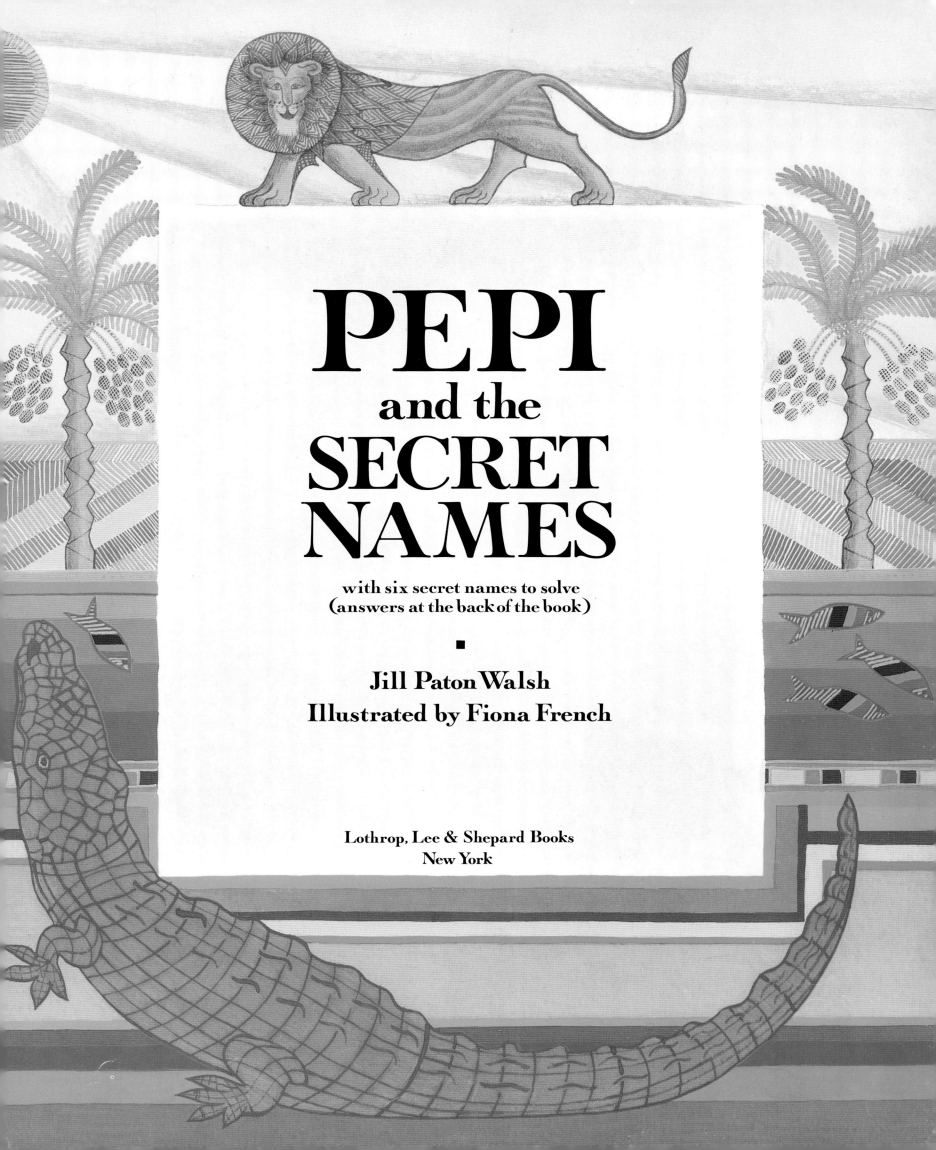

PEPI
and the
SECRET
NAMES

with six secret names to solve
(answers at the back of the book)

∎

Jill Paton Walsh
Illustrated by Fiona French

Lothrop, Lee & Shepard Books
New York

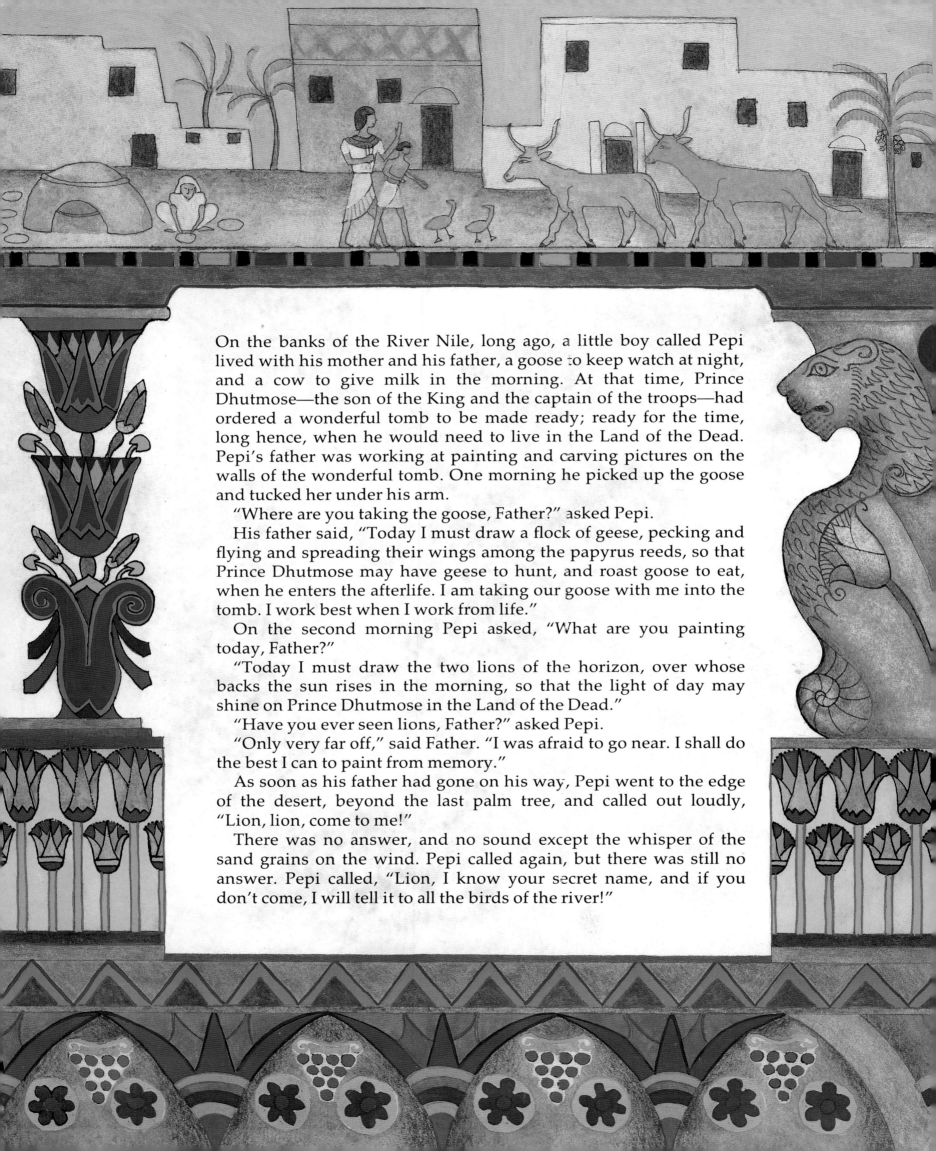

On the banks of the River Nile, long ago, a little boy called Pepi lived with his mother and his father, a goose to keep watch at night, and a cow to give milk in the morning. At that time, Prince Dhutmose—the son of the King and the captain of the troops—had ordered a wonderful tomb to be made ready; ready for the time, long hence, when he would need to live in the Land of the Dead. Pepi's father was working at painting and carving pictures on the walls of the wonderful tomb. One morning he picked up the goose and tucked her under his arm.

"Where are you taking the goose, Father?" asked Pepi.

His father said, "Today I must draw a flock of geese, pecking and flying and spreading their wings among the papyrus reeds, so that Prince Dhutmose may have geese to hunt, and roast goose to eat, when he enters the afterlife. I am taking our goose with me into the tomb. I work best when I work from life."

On the second morning Pepi asked, "What are you painting today, Father?"

"Today I must draw the two lions of the horizon, over whose backs the sun rises in the morning, so that the light of day may shine on Prince Dhutmose in the Land of the Dead."

"Have you ever seen lions, Father?" asked Pepi.

"Only very far off," said Father. "I was afraid to go near. I shall do the best I can to paint from memory."

As soon as his father had gone on his way, Pepi went to the edge of the desert, beyond the last palm tree, and called out loudly, "Lion, lion, come to me!"

There was no answer, and no sound except the whisper of the sand grains on the wind. Pepi called again, but there was still no answer. Pepi called, "Lion, I know your secret name, and if you don't come, I will tell it to all the birds of the river!"

Then a tawny hillock among the sand dunes suddenly moved, and he saw that it was a lion. The lion raised his great shaggy lion's head and roared a slow, deep, broken roar that made Pepi's knees tremble. His tail lifted from the sand and flicked over his great golden back, and he said, "You have threatened me! If it were not so hot, I should eat you for that. Run!"

Pepi trembled, but he stood his ground. "Come with me into the dusty desert tomb where my father is painting the two lions of the horizon, so that he may see you in all your glory and paint well," he said.

"What do I care if he paints well or badly?" said the lion. "And in any case, the two lions of the horizon are god-lions, and I am only a mortal beast."

"Surely not even a god-lion could look more terrifying than you," said Pepi. "And I care whether my father paints well or badly. And I know your secret name; that is why you will come."

The lion yawned a great yawn and said, "Better guess right. I'm a little hungry."

Then Pepi sat down, and he thought about being a great lion in the sandy desert. How good it must be to frighten all your enemies with a single growl!

And Pepi said, "O lion, you are called:

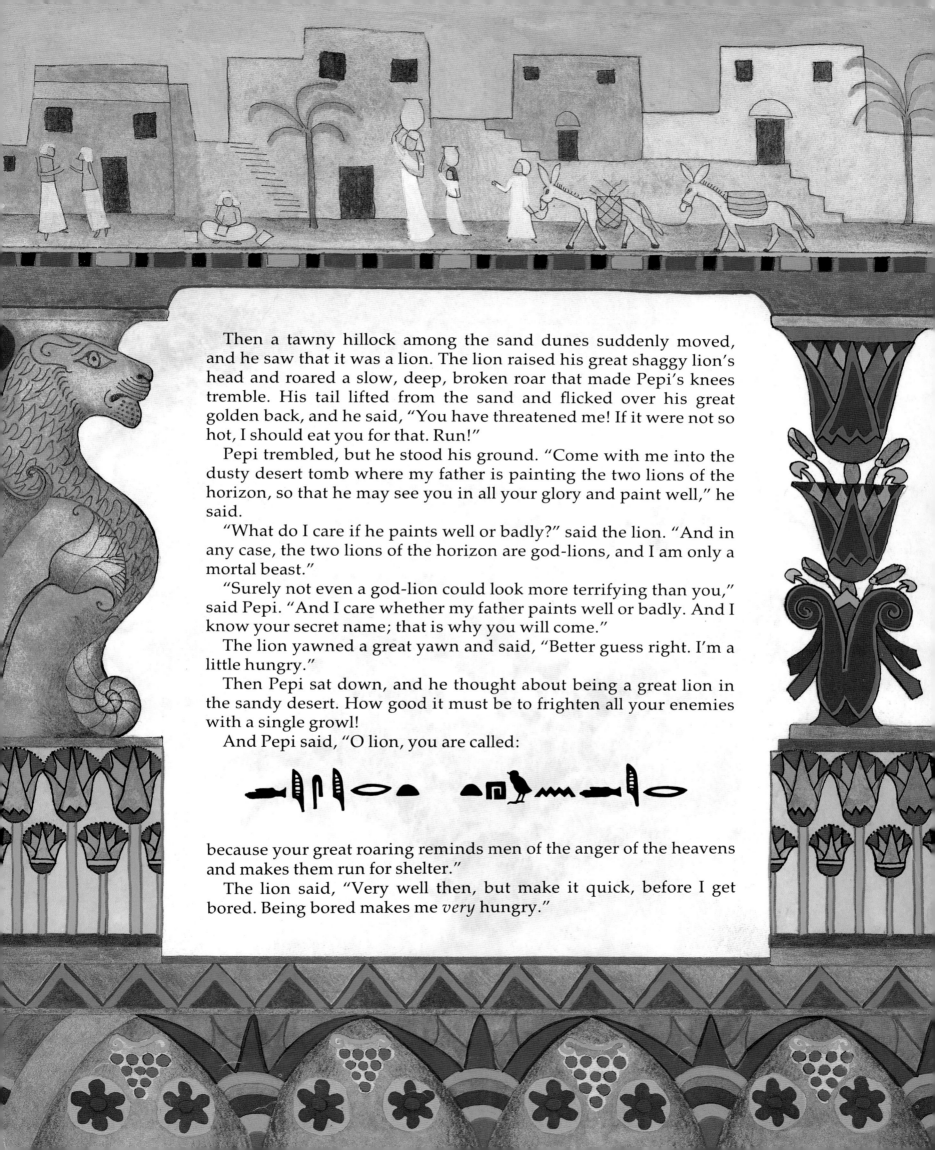

because your great roaring reminds men of the anger of the heavens and makes them run for shelter."

The lion said, "Very well then, but make it quick, before I get bored. Being bored makes me *very* hungry."

So Pepi led the lion up into the desert hills and down the steps into the tomb where the painters were working. Pepi's father went pale as ash when he saw the lion, but the lion growled and said, "Surely the father is not less lionhearted than the son? See, this is how we lie down in the desert when the sun rises over our backs." And he lay down on the floor of the tomb chamber.

Pepi's father painted him looking left, and then he painted him looking right, so that there were the two lions of the horizon, with the sun appearing over their backs in splendor. And while he was working, a little tabby cat came softly in and watched, and somehow the cat got drawn into the picture.

Then the lion said, "I shall return when Prince Dhutmose comes to inspect his tomb, so that he may see how well you have done; and if he is not impressed, I shall eat him, and he will need his tomb that very day!" And with that, the lion went on his way.

The next day Pepi's father told him, "It is a hawk I must paint today—for the god Horus takes the shape of a hawk. He will welcome Prince Dhutmose in the Land of the Dead, and the Prince will worship him there. I have borrowed a tame hawk for today, feather for feather like a wild one."

Pepi went to the riverbank and lay down among the rushes at the water's edge, looking straight up into the endless blue. And by and by he saw a tiny speck wheeling and turning in the tall sky, where a wild hawk hovered high above him.

So he got up and called to the hawk, "Hawk, hawk, come to me! I have need of you!" The hawk above him turned in lazy circles and paid no heed.

"Hawk, hawk, by your secret name I conjure you!" cried Pepi.

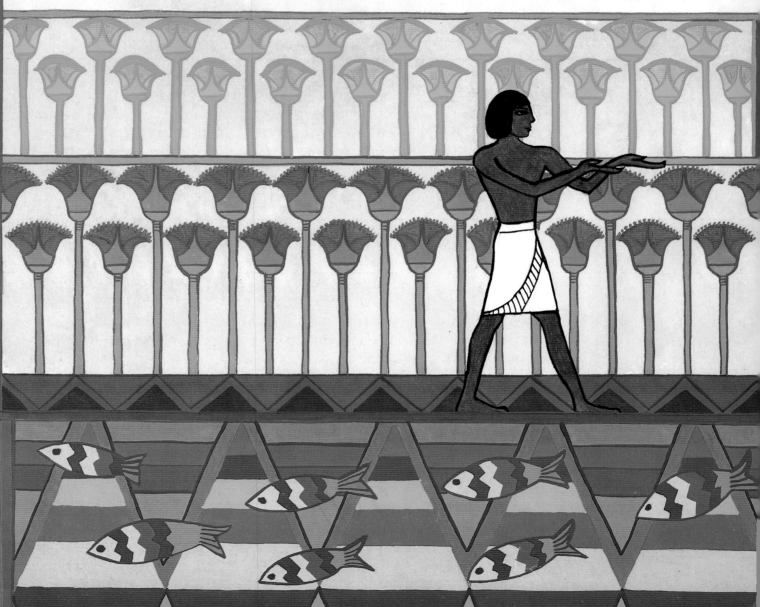

The hawk dropped like a stone out of the air and landed so close to Pepi that he felt a sweep of air from its wings. Then, wings folded, the great bird stood and stared with anger in its fierce and golden eyes. "If you call me by my name and you do not know it, I will peck out your eyes," it said. "And you cannot know it."

Pepi was very frightened, but he thought hard about what hawks do. "You are called Thunderbolt of Death," he said, "because you fall from above upon small creeping things on the face of the earth."

"I do," said the hawk. "I hunt to live. All things under the sun take what they need to live. But neither thunderbolt nor death is in my true name."

Then Pepi wondered for a moment what it was like to be the hawk, gliding only a little below the sun.

He said, "O hawk, you are called:

because nothing is hidden from you on the face of the earth."

And the hawk said, "You know me. What do you want with me?"

"Today," said Pepi, "my father is painting Horus, the hawk god, your master, on the walls of a tomb for Prince Dhutmose. And he has only a tame hawk to show him what a hawk is like. Feather for feather, he will paint well . . ."

"The truth of me is more like flame than feathers," said the hawk scornfully.

"Can Prince Dhutmose worship feathers in the Land of the Dead?" asked Pepi. "Come with me and let my father paint you as a god."

Then the hawk flew up from the ground and settled on Pepi's shoulder, gripping hard with its sharp, dry claws. And Pepi carried it up the dusty road to the valley of the tombs and brought it to where his father was working. And the hawk stood proudly on Pepi's shoulders and said to Pepi's father, "Do you value your eyes? Draw me as I am, if you can!"

Pepi's father was afraid. He drew the hawk in its pride and fury, with death burning in its eyes, and with its great wings spread. His fear was in his picture, so that the hawk on the wall was as frightening as the real one on Pepi's shoulder. And while he was working, a little tabby cat came softly in and sat watching, and somehow the cat got drawn into the picture.

"You have eyes worth keeping," said the hawk when it was done. "I shall return when Prince Dhutmose comes to inspect his tomb, so that he can see, if he has eyes, that you have done well." Then Pepi carried the hawk up through the maze of passages and out into the burning heat of the desert valley, and away it flew, and soon it was only a black speck in the dazzling sweep of the sky.

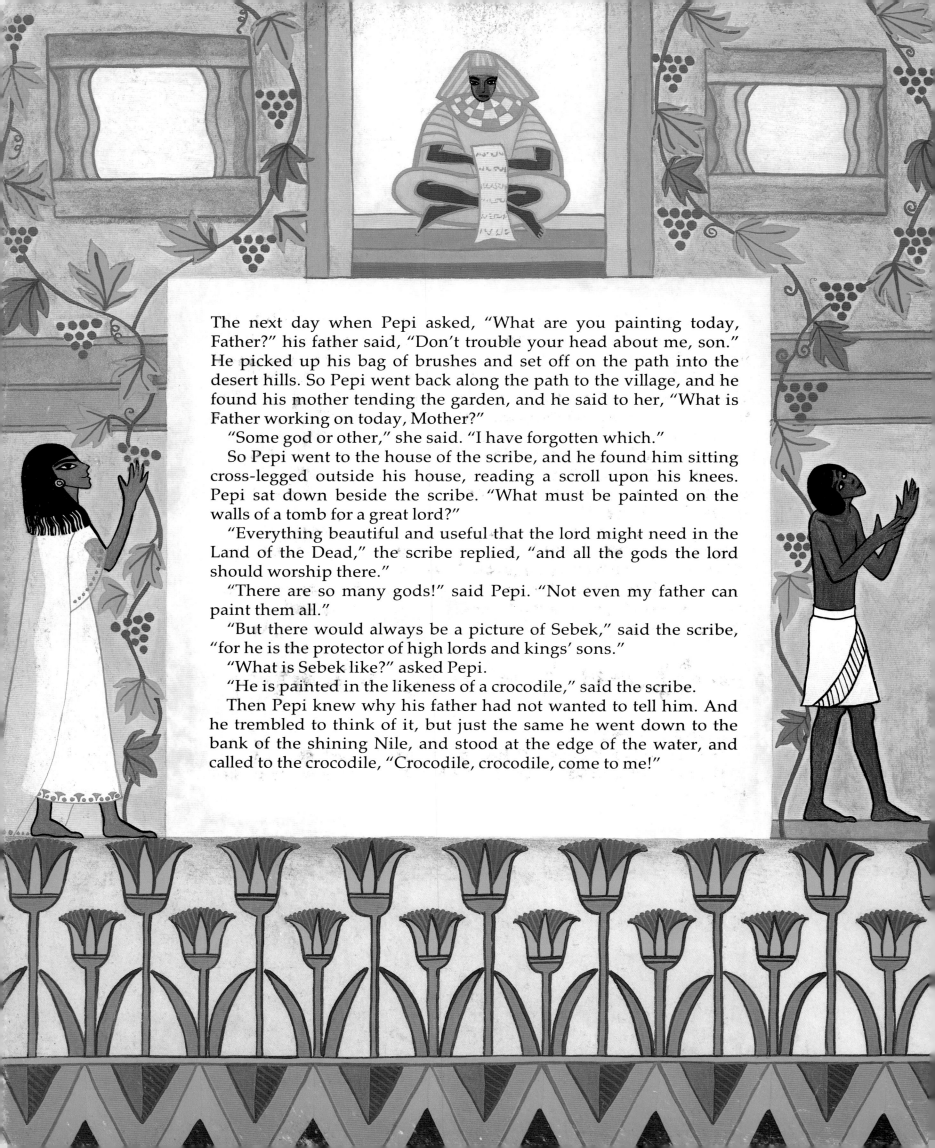

The next day when Pepi asked, "What are you painting today, Father?" his father said, "Don't trouble your head about me, son." He picked up his bag of brushes and set off on the path into the desert hills. So Pepi went back along the path to the village, and he found his mother tending the garden, and he said to her, "What is Father working on today, Mother?"

"Some god or other," she said. "I have forgotten which."

So Pepi went to the house of the scribe, and he found him sitting cross-legged outside his house, reading a scroll upon his knees. Pepi sat down beside the scribe. "What must be painted on the walls of a tomb for a great lord?"

"Everything beautiful and useful that the lord might need in the Land of the Dead," the scribe replied, "and all the gods the lord should worship there."

"There are so many gods!" said Pepi. "Not even my father can paint them all."

"But there would always be a picture of Sebek," said the scribe, "for he is the protector of high lords and kings' sons."

"What is Sebek like?" asked Pepi.

"He is painted in the likeness of a crocodile," said the scribe.

Then Pepi knew why his father had not wanted to tell him. And he trembled to think of it, but just the same he went down to the bank of the shining Nile, and stood at the edge of the water, and called to the crocodile, "Crocodile, crocodile, come to me!"

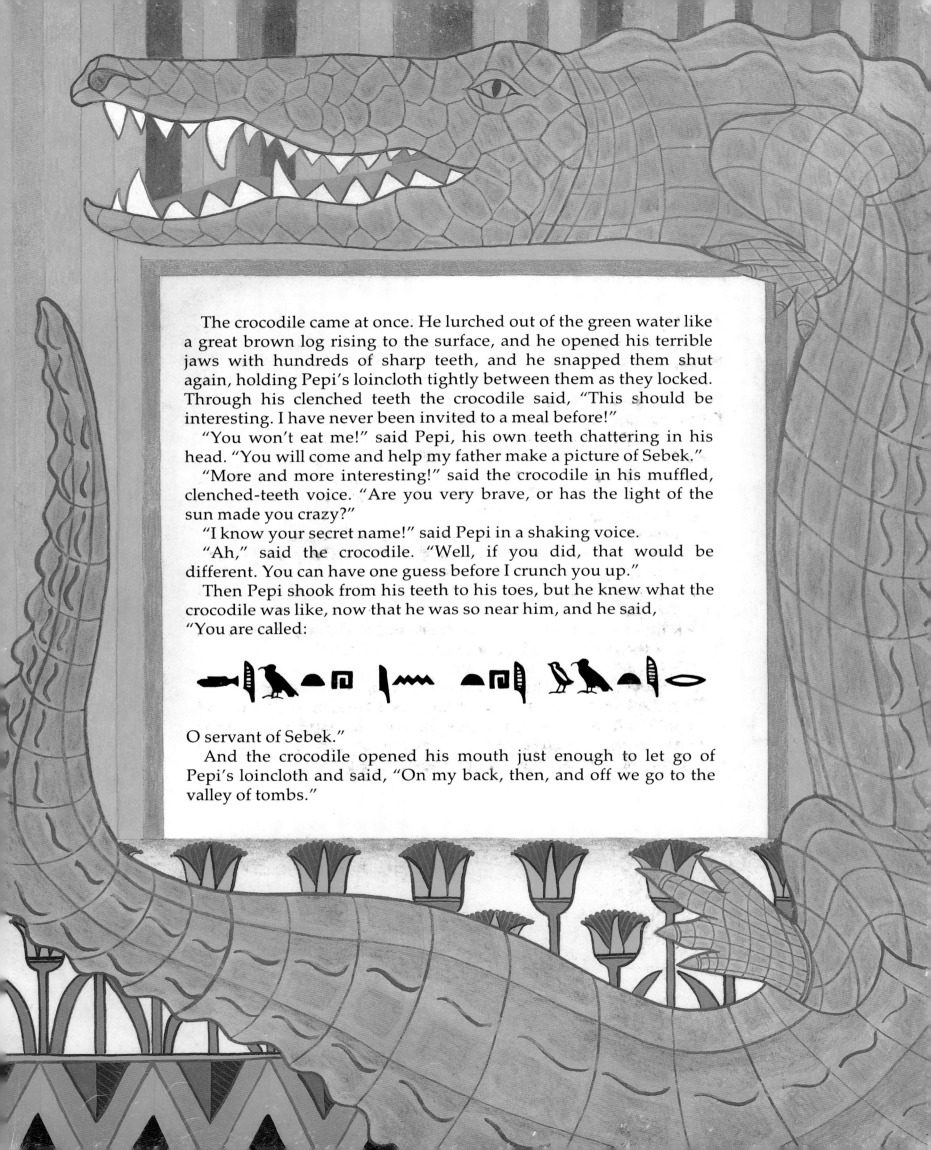

The crocodile came at once. He lurched out of the green water like a great brown log rising to the surface, and he opened his terrible jaws with hundreds of sharp teeth, and he snapped them shut again, holding Pepi's loincloth tightly between them as they locked. Through his clenched teeth the crocodile said, "This should be interesting. I have never been invited to a meal before!"

"You won't eat me!" said Pepi, his own teeth chattering in his head. "You will come and help my father make a picture of Sebek."

"More and more interesting!" said the crocodile in his muffled, clenched-teeth voice. "Are you very brave, or has the light of the sun made you crazy?"

"I know your secret name!" said Pepi in a shaking voice.

"Ah," said the crocodile. "Well, if you did, that would be different. You can have one guess before I crunch you up."

Then Pepi shook from his teeth to his toes, but he knew what the crocodile was like, now that he was so near him, and he said, "You are called:

O servant of Sebek."

And the crocodile opened his mouth just enough to let go of Pepi's loincloth and said, "On my back, then, and off we go to the valley of tombs."

Then Pepi waded into the water and climbed on the crocodile's bumpy back. And off they went, out of the water, up the road, and down the steps into the tomb.

Pepi's father dropped his brushes in his fright at the sight.

"Your son is foolhardy," said the crocodile, "but he guesses well. Work quickly; I will not stay long."

Then Pepi's father drew the head of Sebek, all toothed and terrible like the great beast standing beside him. When it was done, it looked as terrifying as a god should look. While he was working, a little tabby cat came softly in and sat watching. And somehow the cat got drawn, looking at Sebek from behind a palm tree.

"I would like to meet this Dhutmose, of whom so much is told along the riverbank," said the crocodile. "I shall return when he comes to inspect your work, painter, and if he does not like the picture of Sebek, I shall eat him."

"My son," said Pepi's father when the crocodile had begun to walk slowly back to the river, "your help may be the death of this poor painter. There will be a terrible punishment for frightening Prince Dhutmose. Tomorrow you will play at home all day. I command it!"

The next day Pepi found that the gate leading from the little courtyard of his house to the street was bolted, and the bolt was too high for him to reach. So he went and sat beside the gate, in the shade of the archway, and sulked. Suddenly a huge cobra slithered under the gate and reared up close beside him, and in a very quiet, hissing voice it said, "I, too, want to be taken to the tomb in the desert so that your father can draw me from life. Don't make a sound, boy, while I open the gate for you."

Then Pepi said very softly, for he was afraid of the snake, "How do I know my father wants to paint you?"

And the snake said, "Of course he does. He must paint the goddess Mertseger, the cobra with wings, for she protects the desert tombs. I want to be painted living as I am."

"Go by yourself," said Pepi, still whispering. "I am locked in here."

The snake slithered up the gate and curled its head 'round the bolt, drawing it back. Then it slipped down again, and raising its body from the ground, it curled 'round Pepi's shoulders, where it sat and hissed in his ear, "I don't want to go there alone, to be beaten with sticks and bruised with stones by anyone who sees me. You must take me."

Then Pepi was very afraid. "I won't take you anywhere," he said, "unless you tell me your secret name."

And the snake said, "I am called:

but I will not silence you if you will do what I ask."

So Pepi opened the unbarred gate, and he ran as fast as he could into the desert hills, all the way to the tomb entrance. And all the while, he was wearing the snake like a collar, dry and heavy on his bare skin. Down they went, through the maze of chambers and passages, to where Pepi's father was working; and there indeed was the outline of a serpent with hawk's wings, guarding the chamber door.

When Pepi's father looked up and saw his son encircled by the deadly snake, he went as pale as death, but the snake said, "Paint me truly and no harm will come to you, for I have told your son my secret name."

Then Pepi's father drew the snake, once on the left of the door and once on the right; and while he was working, a little tabby cat came softly in and sat watching, and somehow the cat got drawn into the picture.

"The work is done now, and the tomb is finished," said Pepi's father.

And the snake said, "Go home and leave the tomb for me to guard. And when tomorrow Prince Dhutmose comes to see and inspect his tomb, he will find everything just as it should be."

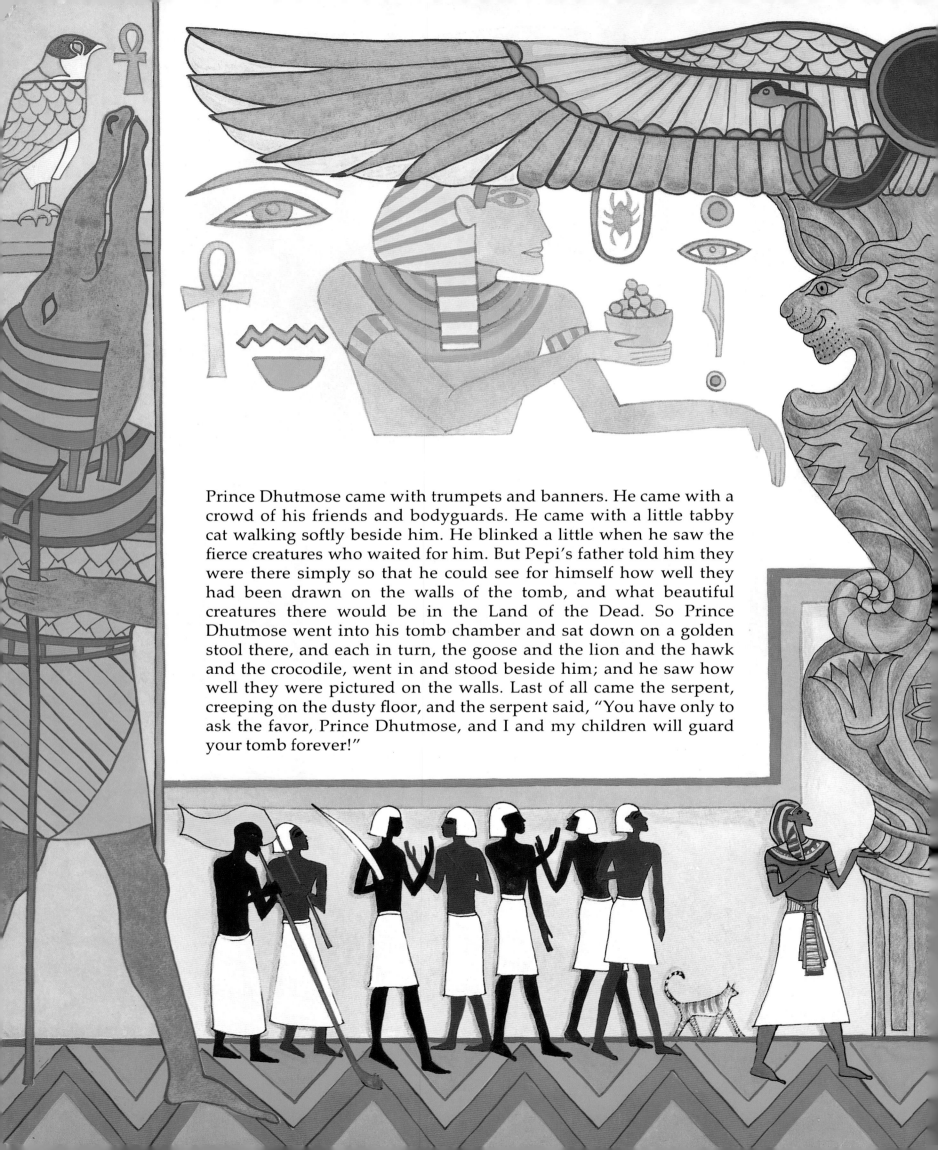

Prince Dhutmose came with trumpets and banners. He came with a crowd of his friends and bodyguards. He came with a little tabby cat walking softly beside him. He blinked a little when he saw the fierce creatures who waited for him. But Pepi's father told him they were there simply so that he could see for himself how well they had been drawn on the walls of the tomb, and what beautiful creatures there would be in the Land of the Dead. So Prince Dhutmose went into his tomb chamber and sat down on a golden stool there, and each in turn, the goose and the lion and the hawk and the crocodile, went in and stood beside him; and he saw how well they were pictured on the walls. Last of all came the serpent, creeping on the dusty floor, and the serpent said, "You have only to ask the favor, Prince Dhutmose, and I and my children will guard your tomb forever!"

"Then, Lord Cobra, I ask that favor of you," said Prince Dhutmose. Turning to Pepi's father, he said, "My tomb is wonderfully painted; my home in the Land of the Dead will be full of the beauty of life. And the Lady Tmiao will stalk in every room, as she does in my home in the land of the living!"

"The Lady Tmiao?" asked Pepi's father.

"My clever cat," said Prince Dhutmose. "She knew I would grieve without her. She will keep me company in my house in the Land of the Dead. But I don't need it yet; I'm not going to die yet. Let us leave this dark desert chamber, and all go to a feast in the garden of my palace, in the shade of my trees, beside my lily pool. Everyone is invited! Come!"

Then Pepi and Pepi's father, and the tomb architect and all the painters, and even the humble diggers and shifters of sand, and all the creatures whose names Pepi had guessed, followed Prince Dhutmose home, and came to the gardens of his palace, and ate and drank and rested in the shade of his trees, while his servants brought food and drink, and his wife and her maidservants sang for them. The Lady Tmiao sat beside the throne of Prince Dhutmose and ate morsels of roast duck from his plate.

And before the party was over, Prince Dhutmose called Pepi and asked him, "How did you make these creatures tame and willing to help your father, little boy?"

"I guessed their secret names," said Pepi.

"You can guess secret names?" said Prince Dhutmose. "Can you guess mine?"

Pepi shook his head. Of all the creatures in the world, he knew least about princes. But just then the Lady Tmiao jumped into Prince Dhutmose's lap, where she sat purring and pressing her paws on his knees.

"Your names are Son of the King, Captain of the Troops, Prince Dhutmose," Pepi said, "but your secret name is:

Prince Dhutmose laughed. "Clever boy!" he said. "You shall have one of her first litter of kittens, and I will send it to you with a collar of lapis and gold!" The Lady Tmiao stared at Pepi with her amber eyes, but she said not a word to him; she only purred.

Egyptian picture writing, called hieroglyphics, is one of the oldest and most beautiful forms of writing. Hieroglyphics used three kinds of signs, many of which were little pictures of creatures or objects: 1.) alphabetic signs, which stood for sounds in the ancient Egyptian language, 2.) syllabic signs, which stood for syllables, and 3.) picture signs, which helped people read the words (for example, a picture of a woman might be drawn beside the word for woman). The names of important people were often enclosed in an oval frame called a cartouche. Because some of the signs represented sounds and were used like the letters of our alphabet, it is possible, just for fun, to write English words using hieroglyphics.

Here are the secret names made plain for you:

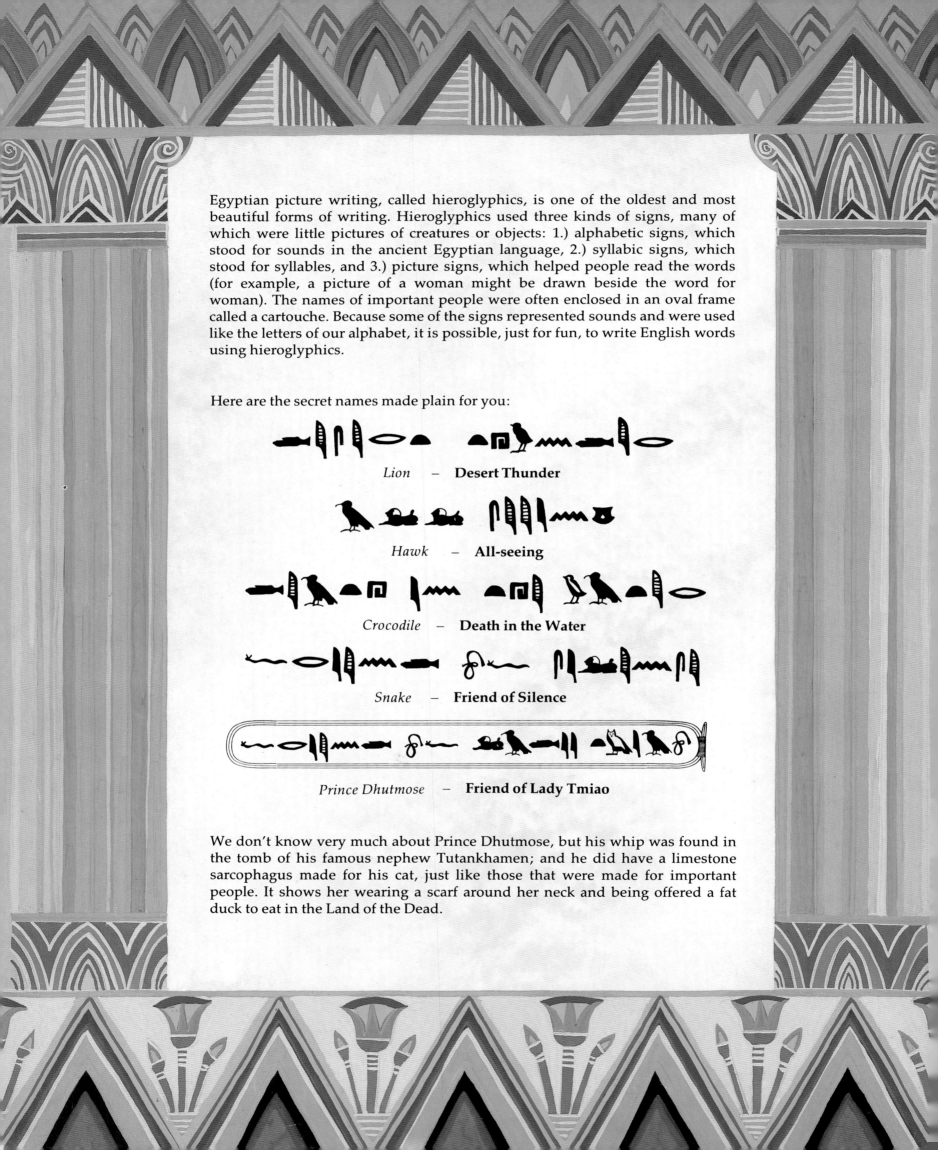

Lion — **Desert Thunder**

Hawk — **All-seeing**

Crocodile — **Death in the Water**

Snake — **Friend of Silence**

Prince Dhutmose — **Friend of Lady Tmiao**

We don't know very much about Prince Dhutmose, but his whip was found in the tomb of his famous nephew Tutankhamen; and he did have a limestone sarcophagus made for his cat, just like those that were made for important people. It shows her wearing a scarf around her neck and being offered a fat duck to eat in the Land of the Dead.

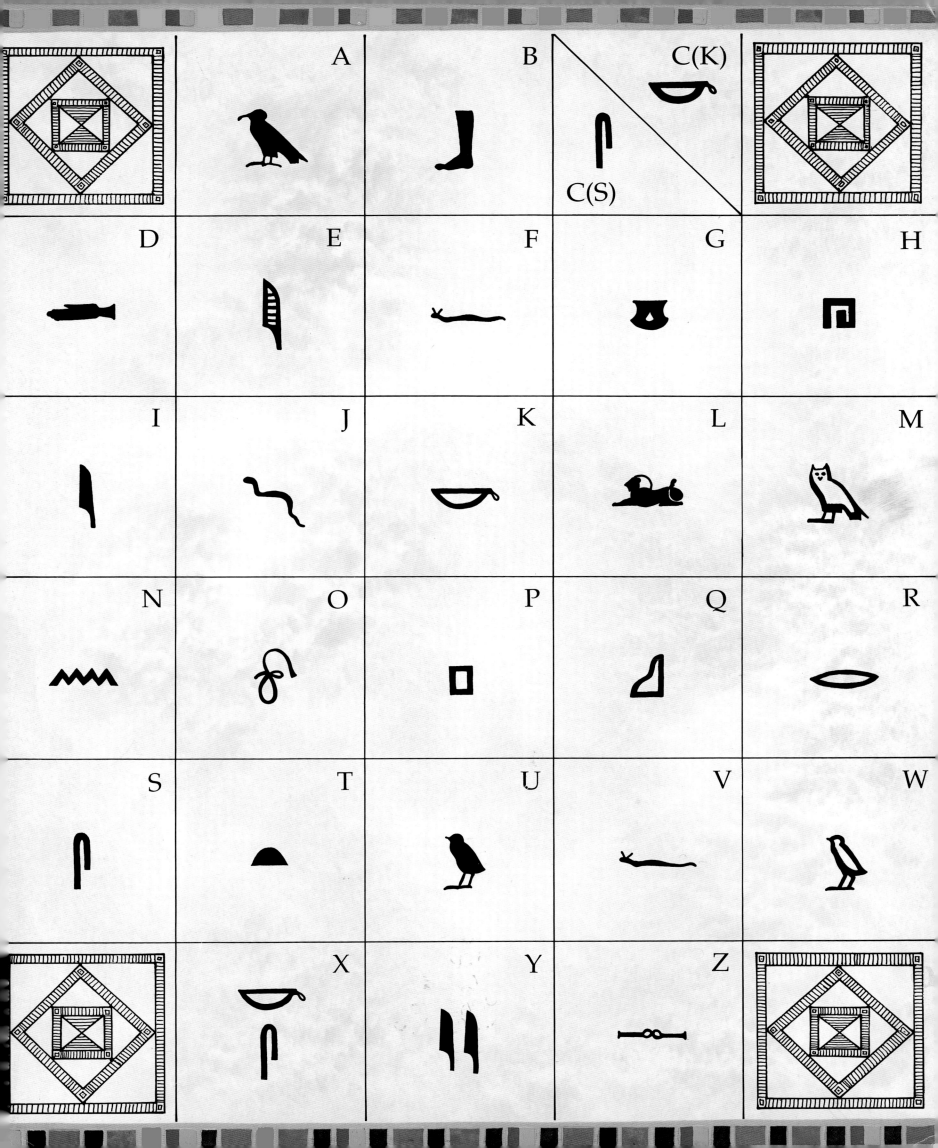

Egypt: Hawks
cats   lions